THE THREE WISHES

BY

WILLIAM CARLETON

British Library Cataloguing-in-Publication Data
A catalogue record for this book is available from
the British Library

Contents

Page
No.

WILLIAM CARLETON

William Carleton was born in Prillisk, Clogher, Northern Ireland in 1794. His father was a tenant farmer, and Carleton received a basic education, moving between various hedge schools. He initially worked as a teacher, before moving to Dublin, and in the late 1820s began to publish written work. 'The Pilgrimage to Lough Derg,' published in the *Christian Examiner*, attracted great attention, and two years later Carleton's *Traits and Stories of the Irish Peasantry* (1830, 2 vols.) placed him amongst the best Irish novelists writing at that time. Over the course of the rest of his life, Carleton wrote constantly, producing a number of well-read novels such as *Valentine* McClutchy (3 vols., 1845), *The Black Prophet, a Tale of Irish Famine* (1846), *The Emigrants of Ahadarra* (1847),*Willy Reilly and his dear Cooleen Bawn* (1850) and *The Tithe Proctor* (1849). He also produced a good amount of short fiction. Carleton died in Sandford, Ireland in 1869.

THE THREE WISHES

William Carleton

In ancient times there lived a man called Billy Dawson, and he was known to be a great rogue. They say he was descended from the family of the Dawsons, which was the reason, I suppose, of his carrying their name upon him.

Billy, in his youthful days, was the best hand at doing nothing in all Europe; devil a mortal could come next or near him at idleness; and, in consequence of his great practice that way, you may be sure that if any man could make a fortune by it he would have done it.

Billy was the only son of his father, barring two daughters, but they have nothing to do with the story I'm telling you. Indeed it was kind father and grandfather for Billy to be handy at the knavery as well as at the idleness, for it was well known that not one of their blood ever did an honest act, except with a roguish intention. In short, they were altogether a *dacent* connection and a credit to the name. As for Billy, all the villainy of the family, both plain and ornamental, came down to him by way of legacy, for it so happened that the father, in spite of all his cleverness, had nothing but his roguery to *lave* him.

Billy, to do him justice, improved the fortune he got. Every day advanced him farther into dishonesty and poverty, until, at the long run, he was acknowledged on all hands to be the completest swindler and the poorest vagabond in the whole parish.

Billy's father, in his young days, had often been forced to acknowledge the inconvenience of not having a trade, in

2

consequence of some nice point in law, called the 'Vagrant Act,' that sometimes troubled him. On this account he made up his mind to give Bill an occupation, and he accordingly bound him to a blacksmith; but whether Bill was to *live* or *die* by *forgery* was a puzzle to his father—though the neighbors said that *both* was most likely. At all events, he was put apprentice to a smith for seven years, and a hard card his master had to play in managing him. He took the proper method, however, for Bill was so lazy and roguish that it would vex a saint to keep him in order.

'Bill,' says his master to him one day that he had been sunning himself about the ditches, instead of minding his business, 'Bill, my boy, I'm vexed to the heart to see you in such a bad state of health. You're very ill with that complaint called an *all-overness*; however,' says he, 'I think I can cure you. Nothing will bring you about but three or four sound doses every day of a medicine called "the oil o' the hazel." Take the first dose now,' says he, and he immediately banged him with a hazel cudgel until Bill's bones ached for a week afterward.

'If you were my son,' said his master, 'I tell you that, as long as I could get a piece of advice growing convenient in the hedges, I'd have you a different youth from what you are. If working was a sin, Bill, not an innocenter boy ever broke bread than you would be. Good people's scarce, you think; but however that may be, I throw it out as a hint, that you must take your medicine till you're cured, whenever you happen to get unwell in the same way.'

From this out he kept Bill's nose to the grinding stone, and whenever his complaint returned he never failed to give him a hearty dose for his improvement.

In the course of time, however, Bill was his own man and his own master, but it would puzzle a saint to know whether the master or the man was the more precious youth in the eyes of the world.

He immediately married a wife, and devil a doubt of it, but if *he* kept *her* in whisky and sugar, *she* kept *him* in hot water. Bill drank and she drank; Bill fought and she fought; Bill was idle and she was idle; Bill whacked her and she whacked Bill. If Bill gave her one black eye, she gave him another, *just to keep herself in countenance*. Never was there a blessed pair so well met, and a beautiful sight it was to see them both at breakfast time, blinking at each other across the potato basket, Bill with his right eye black, and she with her left.

In short, they were the talk of the whole town; and to see Bill of a morning staggering home drunk, his shirt sleeves rolled up on his smutted arms, his breast open, and an old tattered leather apron, with one corner tucked up under his belt, singing one minute and fighting with his wife the next —she, reeling beside him with a discolored eye, as aforesaid, a dirty ragged cap on one side of her head, a pair of Bill's old slippers on her feet, a squalling child on her arm—now cuffing and dragging Bill, and again kissing and hugging him! Yes, it was a pleasant picture to see this loving pair in such a state!

This might do for a while, but it could not last. They were idle, drunken, and ill conducted; and it was not to be supposed that they would get a farthing candle on their words. They were, of course, *dhruv* to great straits; and faith, they soon found that their fighting and drinking and idleness made them the laughing sport of the neighbors; but neither brought food to their *childhre*, put a coat upon their backs, nor satisfied their landlord when he came to look for his own. Still, the never a one of Bill but was a funny fellow with strangers, though, as we said, the greatest rogue unhanged.

One day he was standing against his own anvil, completely in a brown study—being brought to his wit's end how to make out a breakfast for the family. The wife was scolding and cursing in the house, and the naked creatures of children squalling about her knees for food. Bill was fairly at an amplush, and knew not where or how to turn himself, when a poor, withered old beggar came into the forge, tottering on his staff. A long white beard fell from his chin, and he looked as thin and hungry that you might blow him, one would think, over the house. Bill at this moment had been brought to his senses by distress, and his heart had a touch of pity toward the old man, for, on looking at him a second time, he clearly saw starvation and sorrow in his face.

'God save you, honest man!' said Bill.

The old man gave a sigh, and raising himself with great pain on his staff, he looked at Bill in a very beseeching way.

'Musha, God save you kindly!' says he. 'Maybe you could give a poor, hungry, helpless ould man a mouthful of something to ait? You see yourself I'm not able to work; if I was, I'd scorn to be beholding to anyone.'

'Faith, honest man,' said Bill, 'if you knew who you're speaking to, you'd as soon ask a monkey for a churnstaff as me for either mate or money. There's not a blackguard in the three kingdoms so fairly on the *shaughran* as I am for both the one and the other. The wife within is sending the curses thick and heavy on me, and the *childhre's* playing the cat's melody to keep her in comfort. Take my word for it, poor man, if I had either mate or money I'd help you, for I know particularly well what it is to want them at the present speaking; an empty sack won't stand, neighbor.'

So far Bill told him truth. The good thought was in his heart, because he found himself on a footing with the beggar; and nothing brings down pride, or softens the heart, like feeling what it is to want.

'Why, you are in a worse state than I am,' said the old man; 'you have a family to provide for, and I have only myself to support.'

'You may kiss the book on that, my old worthy,' replied Bill; 'but come, what I can do for you I will; plant yourself up here beside the fire, and I'll give it a blast or two of my bellows that will warm the old blood in your body. It's a cold, miserable, snowy day, and a good heat will be of service.'

'Thank you kindly,' said the old man; 'I *am* cold, and a

warming at your fire will do me good, sure enough. Oh, but it *is* a bitter, bitter day; God bless it!'

He then sat down, and Bill blew a rousing blast that soon made the stranger edge back from the heat. In a short time he felt quite comfortable, and when the numbness was taken out of his joints, he buttoned himself up and prepared to depart.

'Now,' says he to Bill, 'you hadn't the food to give me, but *what you could you did*. Ask any three wishes you choose, and be they what they may, take my word for it, they shall be granted.'

Now, the truth is, that Bill, though he believed himself a great man in point of 'cuteness, wanted, after all, a full quarter of being square, for there is always a great difference between a wise man and a knave. Bill was so much of a rogue that he could not, for the blood of him, ask an honest wish, but stood scratching his head in a puzzle.

'Three wishes!' said he. 'Why, let me see—did you say *three?*'

'Ay,' replied the stranger, 'three wishes—that was what I said.'

'Well,' said Bill, 'here goes—aha!—let me alone, my old worthy!—faith I'll overreach the parish, if what you say is true. I'll cheat them in dozens, rich and poor, old and young; let me alone, man—I have it here,' and he tapped his fore- head with great glee. 'Faith, you're the sort to meet of a frosty morning, when a man wants his breakfast; and I'm sorry that I have neither money nor credit to get a bottle of whisky, that we might take our *morning* together.'

'Well, but let us hear the wishes,' said the old man; 'my time is short, and I cannot stay much longer.'

'Do you see this sledge hammer?' said Bill. 'I wish, in the first place, that whoever takes it up in their hands may never be able to lay it down till I give them lave; and that whoever begins to sledge with it may never stop sledging till it's my pleasure to release him.

'Secondly—I have an armchair, and I wish that whoever

sits down in it may never rise out of it till they have my consent.

'And, thirdly—that whatever money I put into my purse, nobody may have power to take it out of it but myself!'

'You Devil's rip!' says the old man in a passion, shaking his staff across Bill's nose. 'Why did you not ask something that would sarve you both here and hereafter? Sure it's as common as the market cross, that there's not a vagabone in His Majesty's dominions stands more in need of both.'

'Oh! By the elevens,' said Bill, 'I forgot that altogether! Maybe you'd be civil enough to let me change one of them? The sorra purtier wish ever was made than I'll make, if only you'll give me another chance at it.'

'Get out, you reprobate,' said the old fellow, still in a passion. 'Your day of grace is past. Little you knew who was speaking to you all this time. I'm St Moroky, you black-guard, and I gave you an opportunity of doing something for yourself and your family; but you neglected it, and now your fate is cast, you dirty, bog-trotting profligate. Sure, it's well known what you are! Aren't you a byword in every-body's mouth, you and your scold of a wife? By this and by that, if ever you happen to come across me again, I'll send you to where you won't freeze, you villain!'

He then gave Bill a rap of his cudgel over the head and laid him at his length beside the bellows, kicked a broken coal scuttle out of his way, and left the forge in a fury.

When Billy recovered himself from the effects of the blow and began to think on what had happened, he could have quartered himself with vexation for not asking great wealth as one of the wishes at least; but now the die was cast on him, and he could only make the most of the three he pitched upon.

He now bethought him how he might turn them to the best account, and here his cunning came to his aid. He began by sending for his wealthiest neighbors on pretence of busi-ness, and when he got them under his roof he offered them the armchair to sit down in. He now had them safe, nor could all the art of man relieve them except worthy Bill was willing. Bill's plan was to make the best bargain he could before he released his prisoners; and let him alone for knowing how to make their purses bleed. There wasn't a wealthy man in the country he did not fleece. The parson of the parish bled heavily; so did the lawyer; and a rich attorney, who had retired from practice, swore that the Court of Chancery itself was paradise compared to Bill's chair.

This was all very good for a time. The fame of his chair, however, soon spread; so did that of his sledge. In a short time neither man, woman, nor child would darken his door; all avoided him and his fixtures as they would a spring gun or mantrap. Bill, so long as he fleeced his neighbors, never wrought a hand's turn; so that when his money was out he found himself as badly off as ever. In addition to all this, his character was fifty times worse than before, for it was the general belief that he had dealings with the old boy. Nothing now could exceed his misery, distress, and ill temper. The wife and he and their children all fought among one another. Everybody hated them, cursed them, and avoided them. The people thought they were acquainted with more than Christian people ought to know. This, of course, came to Bill's ears, and it vexed him very much.

One day he was walking about the fields, thinking of how he could raise the wind once more; the day was dark, and he found himself, before he stopped, in the bottom of a lonely glen covered by great bushes that grew on each side. 'Well,' thought he, when every other means of raising money failed him, 'it's reported that I'm in league with the old boy, and as it's a folly to have the name of the connection without the profit, I'm ready to make a bargain with him any day—so,' said he, raising his voice, 'Nick, you sinner, if you be convanient and willing, why stand out here; show your best leg—here's your man.'

The words were hardly out of his mouth when a dark, sober-looking old gentleman, not unlike a lawyer, walked up to him. Bill looked at the foot and saw the hoof. 'Morrow, Nick,' says Bill.

'Morrow, Bill,' says Nick. 'Well, Bill, what's the news?'

'Devil a much myself hears of late,' says Bill; 'is there anything *fresh* below?'

'I can't exactly say, Bill; I spend little of my time down now; the Tories are in office, and my hands are consequently too full of business here to pay much attention to anything else.'

'A fine place this, sir,' says Bill, 'to take a constitutional walk in; when I want an appetite I often come this way myself—hem! *High* feeding is very bad without exercise.'

'High feeding! Come, come, Bill, you know you didn't taste a morsel these four-and-twenty hours.'

'You know that's a bounce, Nick. I eat a breakfast this morning that would put a stone of flesh on you, if you only smelt at it.'

'No matter; this is not to the purpose. What's that you were muttering to yourself a while ago? If you want to come to the brunt, here I'm for you.'

'Nick,' said Bill, 'you're complate; you want nothing barring a pair of Brian O'Lynn's breeches.'

Bill, in fact, was bent on making his companion open the bargain, because he had often heard that, in that case, with proper care on his own part, he might defeat him in the long run. The other, however, was his match.

'What was the nature of Brian's garment?' inquired Nick.

'Why, you know the song,' said Bill:

> '*Brian O'Lynn had no breeches to wear,*
> *So he got a sheep's skin for to make him a pair;*
> *With the fleshy side out and the woolly side in,*
> *"They'll be pleasant and cool," says Brian O'Lynn.*

'A *cool* pare would sarve you, Nick.'

'You're mighty waggish today, Misther Dawson.'

'And good right I have,' said Bill; 'I'm a man snug and

well to do in the world; have lots of money, plenty of good eating and drinking, and what more need a man wish for?'

'True,' said the other; 'in the meantime it's rather odd that so respectable a man should not have six inches of unbroken cloth in his apparel. You're as naked a tatterdemalion as I ever laid my eyes on; in full dress for a party of scarecrows, William?'

'That's my own fancy, Nick; I don't work at my trade like a gentleman. This is my forge dress, you know.'

'Well, but what did you summon me here for?' said the other; 'you may as well speak out, I tell you, for, my good friend, unless *you* do, *I* shan't. Smell that.'

'I smell more than that,' said Bill; 'and by the way, I'll thank you to give me the windy side of you—curse all sulphur, I say. There, that's what I call an improvement in my condition. But as you *are* so stiff,' says Bill, 'why, the short and long of it is—that—ahem—you see I'm—tut—sure you know I have a thriving trade of my own, and that if I like I needn't be at a loss; but in the meantime I'm rather in a kind of a so—so—don't you *take?*'

And Bill winked knowingly, hoping to trick him into the first proposal.

'You must speak aboveboard, my friend,' says the other. 'I'm a man of few words, blunt and honest. If you have anything to say, be plain. Don't think I can be losing my time with such a pitiful rascal as you are.'

'Well,' says Bill. 'I want money, then, and am ready to come into terms. What have you to say to that, Nick?'

'Let me see—let me look at you,' says his companion, turning him about. 'Now, Bill, in the first place, are you not as finished a scarecrow as ever stood upon two legs?'

'I play second fiddle to you there again,' says Bill.

'There you stand, with the blackguards' coat of arms quartered under your eye, and—'

'Don't make little of *black*guards,' said Bill, 'nor spake disparagingly of *your own* crest.'

'Why, what would you bring, you brazen rascal, if you were fairly put up at auction?'

'Faith, I'd bring more bidders than you would,' said Bill, 'if you were to go off at auction tomorrow. I tell you they should bid *downward* to come to your value, Nicholas. We have no coin *small* enough to purchase you.'

'Well, no matter,' said Nick. 'If you are willing to be mine at the expiration of seven years, I will give you more money than ever the rascally breed of you was worth.'

'Done!' said Bill. 'But no disparagement to my family, in the meantime; so down with the hard cash, and don't be a *neger*.'

The money was accordingly paid down; but as nobody was present, except the giver and receiver, the amount of what Bill got was never known.

'Won't you give me a luck penny?' said the old gentleman.

'Tut,' said Billy, 'so prosperous an old fellow as you cannot want it; however, bad luck to you, with all my heart! and it's rubbing grease to a fat pig to say so. Be off now, or I'll commit suicide on you. Your absence is a cordial to most people, you infernal old profligate. You have injured my morals even for the short time you have been with me, for I don't find myself so virtuous as I was.'

'Is that your gratitude, Billy?'

'Is it gratitude *you* speak of, man? I wonder you don't blush when you name it. However, when you come again, if you bring a third eye in your head you will see what I mane, Nicholas, ahagur.'

The old gentleman, as Bill spoke, hopped across the ditch on his way to *Downing* Street, where of late 'tis thought he possesses much influence.

Bill now began by degrees to show off, but still wrought a little at his trade to blindfold the neighbors. In a very short time, however, he became a great man. So long indeed as he was a *poor* rascal, no decent person would speak to him; even the proud servingmen at the 'Big House' would turn up their noses at him. And he well deserved to be made little of by others, because he was mean enough to make little of himself. But when it was seen and known that he had oceans of money, it was wonderful to think, although he was *now* a greater blackguard than ever, how those who despised him before began to come round him and court his company. Bill, however, had neither sense nor spirit to make those sunshiny friends know their distance; not he—instead of that he was proud to be seen in decent company, and so long as the money lasted, it was 'hail fellow well met' between himself and every fair-faced *spunger* who had a horse under him, a decent coat to his back, and a good appetite to eat his dinners. With riches and all, Bill was the same man still; but, somehow or other, there is a great difference between a rich profligate and a poor one, and Bill found it so to his cost in *both* cases.

Before half the seven years was passed, Bill had his carriage and his equipages; was hand and glove with my Lord This, and my Lord That; kept hounds and hunters; was the first sportsman at the Curragh; patronised every boxing ruffian he could pick up; and betted night and day on cards, dice, and horses. Bill, in short, *should* be a blood, and except he did all this, he could not presume to mingle with the fashionable bloods of his time.

It's an old proverb, however, that 'what is got over the Devil's back is sure to go off under it,' and in Bill's case this proved true. In short, the old boy himself could not supply him with money so fast as he made it fly; it was 'come easy, go easy,' with Bill, and so sign was on it, before he came within two years of his time he found his purse empty.

And now came the value of his summer friends to be known. When it was discovered that the cash was no longer flush with him—that stud, and carriage, and hounds were going to the hammer—whish! off they went, friends, relations, pot companions, dinner eaters, black-legs, and all, like a flock of crows that had smelt gunpowder. Down Bill soon went, week after week and day after day, until at last he was obliged to put on the leather apron and take to the hammer again; and not only that, for as no experience could make him wise, he once more began his taproom brawls, his quarrels with Judy, and took to his 'high feeding' at the dry potatoes and salt. Now, too, came the cutting tongues of all who knew him, like razors upon him. Those that he scorned because they were poor and himself rich now paid him back his own with interest; and those that he had measured himself with, because they were rich, and who only countenanced him in consequence of his wealth, gave him the hardest word in their cheeks. The Devil mend him! He deserved it all, and more if he had got it.

Bill, however, who was a hardened sinner, never fretted himself down an ounce of flesh by what was said to him or of him. Not he; he cursed, and fought, and swore, and schemed away as usual, taking in everyone he could; and surely none could match him at villainy of all sorts and sizes.

At last the seven years became expired, and Bill was one morning sitting in his forge, sober and hungry, the wife cursing him, and the children squalling as before; he was thinking how he might defraud some honest neighbour out of a breakfast to stop their mouths and his own, too, when who walks in to him but old Nick to demand his bargain.

'Morrow, Bill!' says he with a sneer.

'The Devil welcome you!' says Bill. 'But you have a fresh memory.'

'A bargain's a bargain between two *honest* men, any day,' says Satan; 'when I speak of *honest* men, I mean *yourself* and *me*, Bill'; and he put his tongue in his cheek to make game of the unfortunate rogue he had come for.

'Nick, my worthy fellow,' said Bill, 'have bowels; you wouldn't do a shabby thing; you wouldn't disgrace your own character by putting more weight upon a falling man. You know what it is to get a *comedown* yourself, my worthy; so just keep your toe in your pump, and walk off with yourself somewhere else. A *cool* walk will sarve you better than my company, Nicholas.'

'Bill, it's no use in shirking,' said his friend; 'your

swindling tricks may enable you to cheat others, but you won't cheat *me*, I guess. You want nothing to make you perfect in your way but to travel; and travel you shall under my guidance, Billy. No, no—I'm not to be swindled, my good fellow. I have rather a—a—better opinion of myself, Mr D., than to think that you could outwit one Nicholas Clutie, Esq.—ahem!'

'You may sneer, you sinner,' replied Bill, 'but I tell you that I have outwitted men who could buy and sell you to your face. Despair, you villain, when I tell you that *no attorney* could stand before me.'

Satan's countenance got blank when he heard this; he wriggled and fidgeted about and appeared to be not quite comfortable.

'In that case, then,' says he, 'the sooner I *deceive* you the better; so turn out for the *Low Countries*.'

'Is it come to that in earnest?' said Bill. 'And are you going to act the rascal at the long run?'

''Pon honor, Bill.'

'Have patience, then, you sinner, till I finish this horse-shoe—it's the last of a set I'm finishing for one of your friend the attorney's horses. And here, Nick, I hate idleness; you know it's the mother of mischief; take this sledge hammer and give a dozen strokes or so, till I get it out of hands, and then here's with you, since it must be so.'

He then gave the bellows a puff that blew half a peck of dust in Club-foot's face, whipped out the red-hot iron, and set Satan sledging away for bare life.

'Faith,' says Bill to him, when the shoe was finished, 'it's a thousand pities ever the sledge should be out of your hand; the great *Parra Gow* was a child to you at sledging, you're such an able tyke. Now just exercise yourself till I bid the wife and childhre good-by, and then I'm off.'

Out went Bill, of course, without the slightest notion of coming back; no more than Nick had that he could not give up the sledging, and indeed neither could he, but was forced to work away as if he was sledging for a wager. This was just what Bill wanted. He was now compelled to sledge on until it was Bill's pleasure to release him; and so we leave him very industriously employed, while we look after the worthy who outwitted him.

In the meantime Bill broke cover and took to the country at large; wrought a little journey work wherever he could get it, and in this way went from one place to another, till, in the course of a month, he walked back very coolly into his own forge to see how things went on in his absence. There he found Satan in a rage, the perspiration pouring from him in torrents, hammering with might and main upon the naked anvil. Bill calmly leaned back against the wall, placed his hat upon the side of his head, put his hands into his breeches pockets, and began to whistle *Shaun Gow's* hornpipe. At length he says, in a very quiet and good-humored way:

'Morrow, Nick!'

'Oh!' says Nick, still hammering away. 'Oh! you double-distilled villain (hech!), may the most refined, ornamental (hech!) collection of curses that ever was gathered (hech!) into a single nosegay of ill fortune (hech!) shine in the buttonhole of your conscience (hech!) while your name is Bill Dawson! I denounce you (hech!) as a doublemilled villain, a finished, hot-pressed knave (hech!), in comparison of whom all the other knaves I ever knew (hech!), attorneys included, are honest men. I brand you (hech!) as the pearl of cheats, a tiptop take-in (hech!). I denounce you, I say again, for the villainous treatment (hech!) I have received at your hands in this most untoward (hech!) and unfortunate transaction between us; for (hech!) unfortunate, in every sense, is he that has anything to do with (hech!) such a prime and finished impostor.'

'You're very warm, Nicky,' says Bill; 'what puts you into a passion, you old sinner? Sure if it's your own will and pleasure to take exercise at my anvil, *I'm* not to be abused for it. Upon my credit, Nicky, you ought to blush for using such blackguard language, so unbecoming your grave character. You cannot say that it was I set you a-hammering at the empty anvil, you profligate.

'However, as you are so very industrious, I simply say it would be a thousand pities to take you from it. Nick, I love industry in my heart, and I always encourage it, so work away; it's not often you spend your time so creditably. I'm afraid if you weren't at that you'd be worse employed.'

'Bill, have bowels,' said the operative; 'you wouldn't go to lay more weight on a falling man, you know; you wouldn't disgrace your character by such a piece of iniquity as keeping an inoffensive gentleman advanced in years, at such an unbecoming and rascally job as this. Generosity's your top virtue, Bill; not but that you have many other excellent ones, as well as that, among which, as you say yourself, I reckon industry; but still it is in generosity you *shine*. Come, Bill, honor bright, and release me.'

'Name the terms, you profligate.'

'You're above terms, William; a generous fellow like you never thinks of terms.'

'Good-by, old gentleman!' said Bill very coolly. 'I'll drop in to see you once a month.'

'No, no, Bill, you infern—a—a—. You excellent, worthy, delightful fellow, not so fast; not so fast. Come, name your terms, you sland—My dear Bill, name your terms.'

'Seven years more.'

'I agree; but—'

'And the same supply of cash as before, down on the nail here.'

'Very good; very good. You're rather simple, Bill; rather soft, I must confess. Well, no matter. I shall yet turn the tab —a—hem! You are an exceedingly simple fellow, Bill; still there will come a day, my *dear* Bill—there will come—'

'Do you grumble, you vagrant? Another word, and I double the terms.'

'Mum, William—mum; *tace* is Latin for a candle.'

'Seven years more of grace, and the same measure of the needful that I got before. Ay or no?'

'Of grace, Bill! Ay! Ay! Ay! There's the cash. I accept the terms. Oh, blood! The rascal—of grace! Bill!'

'Well, now drop the hammer and vanish,' says Billy; 'but what would you think to take this sledge, while you stay, and give me a—Eh! Why in such a hurry?' he added, seeing that Satan withdrew in double-quick time.

'Hello! Nicholas!' he shouted. 'Come back; you forgot something!' And when the old gentleman looked behind him, Billy shook the hammer at him, on which he vanished altogether.

Billy now got into his old courses; and what shows the kind of people the world is made of, he also took up with his old company. When they saw that he had the money once more and was sowing it about him in all directions, they immediately began to find excuses for his former extravagance.

'Say what you will,' said one, 'Bill Dawson's a spirited fellow that bleeds like a prince.'

'He's a hospitable man in his own house, or out of it, as ever lived,' said another.

'His only fault is,' observed a third, 'that he is, if anything, too generous and doesn't know the value of money; his fault's on the right side, however.'

'He has the spunk in him,' said a fourth; 'keeps a capital table, prime wines, and a standing welcome for his friends.'

'Why,' said a fifth, 'if he doesn't enjoy his money while he lives, he won't when he's dead; so more power to him, and a wider throat to his purse.'

Indeed, the very persons who were cramming themselves at his expense despised him at heart. They knew very well, however, how to take him on the weak side. Praise his generosity, and he would do anything; call him a man of spirit, and you might fleece him to his face. Sometimes he would toss a purse of guineas to this knave, another to that flatterer, a third to a bully, and a fourth to some broken-down rake—and all to convince them that *he* was a sterling friend —a man of mettle and liberality. But never was he known to help a virtuous and struggling family—to assist the widow or the fatherless, or to do any other act that was *truly* useful. It is to be supposed the reason of this was that as he spent it, as most of the world do, in the service of the Devil, by whose aid he got it, he was prevented from turning it to a good account. Between you and me, dear reader, there are more persons acting after Bill's fashion in the same world than you dream about.

When his money was out again, his friends played him the same rascally game once more. No sooner did his poverty become plain than the knaves began to be troubled with small fits of modesty, such as an unwillingness to come to his place when there was no longer anything to be got there. A kind of virgin bashfulness prevented them from speaking to him when they saw him getting out on the wrong side of his clothes. Many of them would turn away from him in the prettiest and most delicate manner when they thought he wanted to borrow money from them—all for fear of putting him to the blush for asking it. Others again, when they saw him coming toward their houses about dinner hour, would become so confused, from mere gratitude, as to think themselves in another place; and their servants, seized, as it were, with the same feeling, would tell Bill that their masters were 'not at home.'

At length, after traveling the same villainous round as before, Bill was compelled to betake himself, as the last remedy, to the forge; in other words, he found that there is, after all, nothing in this world that a man can rely on so firmly and surely as his own industry. Bill, however, wanted the organ of common sense, for his experience—and it was sharp enough to leave an impression—ran off him like water off a duck.

He took to his employment sorely against his grain, but he had now no choice. He must either work or starve, and starvation is like a great doctor—nobody tries it till every other remedy fails them. Bill had been twice rich; twice a gentleman among blackguards, but always a blackguard among gentlemen, for no wealth or acquaintance with decent society could rub the rust of his native vulgarity off him. He was now a common blinking sot in his forge; a drunken bully in the taproom, cursing and browbeating everyone as well as his wife; boasting of how much money he had spent in his day; swaggering about the high doings he carried on; telling stories about himself and Lord This at the Curragh; the dinners he gave—how much they cost him —and attempting to extort credit upon the strength of his former wealth. He was too ignorant, however, to know that he was publishing his own disgrace and that it was a mean-spirited thing to be proud of what ought to make him blush through a deal board nine inches thick.

He was one morning industriously engaged in a quarrel with his wife, who, with a three-legged stool in her hand, appeared to mistake his head for his own anvil; he, in the meantime, paid his addresses to her with his leather apron, when who steps in to jog his memory about the little agreement that was between them but old Nick. The wife, it seems, in spite of all her exertions to the contrary, was getting the worst of it; and Sir Nicholas, willing to appear a gentleman of great gallantry, thought he could not do less than take up the lady's quarrel, particularly as Bill had laid her in a sleeping posture. Now Satan thought this too bad, and as he felt himself under many obligations to the sex, he determined to defend one of them on the present occasion; so as Judy rose, he turned upon her husband and floored him by a clever facer.

'You unmanly villain,' said he, 'is this the way you treat your wife? 'Pon honor Bill, I'll chastise you on the spot. I could not stand by, a spectator of such ungentlemanly conduct, without giving you all claim to gallant—' Whack! The word was divided in his mouth by the blow of a churnstaff from Judy, who no sooner saw Bill struck than she nailed Satan, who 'fell' once more.

'What, you villain! That's for striking my husband like a murderer behind his back,' said Judy, and she suited the action to the word. 'That's for interfering between man and wife. Would you murder the poor man before my face, eh? If *he* bates me, you shabby dog you, who has a better right? I'm sure it's nothing out of your pocket. Must you have your finger in every pie?'

This was anything but *idle* talk, for at every word she gave him a remembrance, hot and heavy. Nicholas backed, danced, and hopped; she advanced, still drubbing him with great perseverance, till at length he fell into the redoubtable armchair, which stood exactly behind him. Bill, who had been putting in two blows for Judy's one, seeing that his enemy was safe, now got between the Devil and his wife, *a situation that few will be disposed to envy him.*

'Tenderness, Judy,' said the husband; 'I hate cruelty. Go put the tongs in the fire, and make them red-hot. Nicholas, you have a nose,' said he.

Satan began to rise but was rather surprised to find that he could not budge.

'Nicholas,' says Bill, 'how is your pulse? You don't look well; that is to say, you look worse than usual.'

The other attempted to rise but found it a mistake.

'I'll thank you to come along,' said Bill. 'I have a fancy to travel under your guidance, and we'll take the *Low Countries* in our way, won't we? Get to your legs, you sinner; you know a bargain's a bargain between two *honest* men, Nicholas, meaning *yourself* and *me*. Judy, are the tongs hot?'

Satan's face was worth looking at as he turned his eyes from the husband to the wife and then fastened them on the tongs, now nearly at a furnace heat in the fire, conscious at the same time that he could not move out of the chair.

'Billy,' said he, 'you won't forget that I rewarded you generously the last time I saw you, in the way of business.'

'Faith, Nicholas, it fails me to remember any generosity I ever showed you. Don't be womanish. I simply want to see what kind of stuff your nose is made of and whether it will stretch like a rogue's conscience. If it does we will flatter it up the *chimly* with red-hot tongs, and when this old hat is fixed on the top of it, let us alone for a weather-cock.'

'Have a *fellow feeling*, Mr Dawson; you know *we* ought not to dispute. Drop the matter, and I give you the next seven years.'

'We know all that,' says Billy, opening the red-hot tongs very coolly.

'Mr Dawson,' said Satan, 'if you cannot remember my friendship to yourself, don't forget how often I stood your father's friend, your grandfather's friend, and the friend of all your relations up to the tenth generation. I intended, also, to stand by your children after you, so long as the name of Dawson—and a respectable one it is—might last.'

'Don't be blushing, Nick,' says Bill; 'you are too modest; that was ever your failing; hould up your head, there's money bid for you. I'll give you such a nose, my good friend, that you will have to keep an outrider before you, to carry the end of it on his shoulder.'

'Mr Dawson, I pledge my honor to raise your children in the world as high as they can go, no matter whether they desire it or not.'

'That's very kind of you,' says the other, 'and I'll do as much for your nose.'

He gripped it as he spoke, and the old boy immediately sung out; Bill pulled, and the nose went with him like a piece of warm wax. He then transferred the tongs to Judy, got a ladder, resumed the tongs, ascended the chimney, and tugged stoutly at the nose until he got it five feet above the roof. He then fixed the hat upon the top of it and came down.

'There's a weathercock,' said Billy; 'I defy Ireland to show such a beauty. Faith, Nick, it would make the purtiest steeple for a church in all Europe, and the old hat fits it to a shaving.'

In this state, with his nose twisted up the chimney, Satan sat for some time, experiencing the novelty of what might be termed a peculiar sensation. At last the worthy husband and wife began to relent.

'I think,' said Bill, 'that we have made the most of the nose, as well as the joke; I believe, Judy, it's long enough.'

'What is?' says Judy.

'Why, the joke,' said the husband.

'Faith, and I think so is the nose,' said Judy.

'What do you say yourself, Satan?' said Bill.

'Nothing at all, William,' said the other; 'but that—ha! ha!—it's a good joke—an excellent joke, and a goodly nose, too, as it *stands*. You were always a gentlemanly man, Bill, and did things with a grace; still, if I might give an opinion on such a trifle—'

'It's no trifle at all,' says Bill, 'if you spake of the nose.'

'Very well, it is not,' says the other; 'still, I am decidedly of opinion that if you could shorten both the joke and the nose without further violence, you would lay me under very heavy obligations, which I shall be ready to acknowledge and *repay* as I ought.'

'Come,' said Bill, 'shell out once more, and be off for seven years. As much as you came down with the last time, and vanish.'

The words were scarcely spoken, when the money was at his feet and Satan invisible. Nothing could surpass the mirth of Bill and his wife at the result of this adventure. They laughed till they fell down on the floor.

It is useless to go over the same ground again. Bill was still incorrigible. The money went as the Devil's money always goes. Bill caroused and squandered but could never turn a penny of it to a good purpose. In this way year after year went, till the seventh was closed and Bill's hour come. He was now, and had been for some time past, as miserable a knave as ever. Not a shilling had he, nor a shilling's worth, with the exception of his forge, his cabin, and a few articles of crazy furniture. In this state he was standing in his forge as before, straining his ingenuity how to make out a breakfast, when Satan came to look after him. The old gentleman was sorely puzzled how to get at him. He kept skulking and sneaking about the forge for some time, till he saw that Bill hadn't a cross to bless himself with. He immediately changed himself into a guinea and lay in an open place where he knew Bill would see him. 'If,' said he, 'I once get into his possession, I can manage him.' The honest smith took the bait, for it was well gilded; he clutched the guinea, put it into his purse, and closed it up. 'Ho! Ho!' shouted the Devil out of the purse. 'You're caught, Bill; I've secured you at last, you knave you. Why don't you despair, you villain, when you think of what's before you?'

'Why, you unlucky ould dog,' said Bill, 'is it there you are? Will you always drive your head into every loophole that's set for you? Faith, Nick achora, I never had you bagged till now.'

Satan then began to tug and struggle with a view of getting out of the purse, but in vain.

'Mr Dawson,' said he, 'we understand each other. I'll give the seven years additional and the cash on the nail.'

'Be aisey, Nicholas. You know the weight of the hammer, that's enough. It's not a whipping with feathers you're going to get, anyhow. Just be aisey.'

'Mr Dawson, I grant I'm not your match. Release me, and I double the case. I was merely trying your temper when I took the shape of a guinea.'

'Faith and I'll try yours before I lave it, I've a notion.' He immediately commenced with the sledge, and Satan sang out with a considerable want of firmness. 'Am I heavy enough?' said Bill.

'Lighter, lighter, William, if you love me. I haven't been well latterly, Mr Dawson—I have been delicate—my health, in short, is in a very precarious state, Mr Dawson.'

'I can believe *that*,' said Bill, 'and it will be more so before I have done with you. Am I doing it right?'

'Bill,' said Nick, 'is this gentlemanly treatment in your own respectable shop? Do you think, if you dropped into my little place, that I'd act this rascally part toward you? Have you no compunction?'

'I know,' replied Bill, sledging away with vehemence, 'that

you're notorious for giving your friends a *warm* welcome. Divil an ould youth more so; but you must be daling in bad coin, must you? However, good or bad, you're in for a sweat now, you sinner. Am I doin' it purty?'

'Lovely, William—but, if possible, a little more delicate.'

'Oh, how delicate you are! Maybe a cup o' tay would sarve you, or a little small gruel to compose your stomach?'

'Mr Dawson,' said the gentleman in the purse, 'hold your hand and let us understand one another. I have a proposal to make.'

'Hear the sinner anyhow,' said the wife.

'Name your own sum,' said Satan, 'only set me free.'

'No, the sorra may take the toe you'll budge till you let Bill off,' said the wife; 'hould him hard, Bill, barrin' he sets *you* clear of your engagement.'

'There it is, my posy,' said Bill; 'that's the condition. If you don't give *me up*, here's at you once more—and you must double the cash you gave the last time, too. So, if you're of that opinion, say *ay*—leave the cash and be off.'

The money appeared in a glittering heap before Bill, upon which he exclaimed, 'The *ay* has it, you dog. Take to your pumps now, and fair weather after you, you vagrant; but, Nicholas—Nick—here, here—' The other looked back and saw Bill, with a broad grin upon him, shaking the purse at him. 'Nicholas, come back,' said he. 'I'm short a guinea.' Nick shook his fist and disappeared.

It would be useless to stop now, merely to inform our readers that Bill was beyond improvement. In short, he once more took to his old habits and lived on exactly in the same manner as before. He had two sons—one as great a blackguard as himself, and who was also named after him; the other was a well-conducted, virtuous young man called James, who left his father and, having relied upon his own industry and honest perseverance in life, arrived afterward to great wealth and built the town called Castle Dawson, which is so called from its founder until this day.

Bill, at length, in spite of all his wealth, was obliged, as he himself said, 'to travel'—in other words, he fell asleep one day and forgot to awaken; or, in still plainer terms, he died.

Now, it is usual, when a man dies, to close the history of his life and adventures at once; but with our hero this cannot be the case. The moment Bill departed he very naturally bent his steps toward the residence of St Moroky, as being, in his opinion, likely to lead him toward the snuggest berth he could readily make out. On arriving, he gave a very humble kind of knock, and St Moroky appeared.

'God save your Reverence!' said Bill, very submissively.

'Be off; there's no admittance here for so poor a youth as you are,' said St Moroky.

He was now so cold and fatigued that he cared like where he went, provided only, as he said himself, 'he could rest his bones and get an air of the fire.' Accordingly, after arriving at a large black gate, he knocked, as before, and was told he would get *instant* admittance the moment he gave his name.

'Billy Dawson,' he replied.

'Off, instantly,' said the porter to his companions, 'and let His Majesty know that the rascal he dreads so much is here at the gate.'

Such a racket and tumult were never heard as the very mention of Billy Dawson created.

In the meantime, his old acquaintance came running toward the gate with such haste and consternation that his tail was several times nearly tripping up his heels.

'Don't admit that rascal,' he shouted; 'bar the gate—make every chain and lock and bolt fast—I won't be safe—and I won't stay here, nor none of us need stay here, if he gets in —my bones are sore yet after him. No, no—begone, you villain—you'll get no entrance here—I know you too well.'

Bill could not help giving a broad, malicious grin at Satan, and, putting his nose through the bars, he exclaimed, 'Ha! You ould dog, I have you afraid of me at last, have I?'

He had scarcely uttered the words, when his foe, who

stood inside, instantly tweaked him by the nose, and Bill felt as if he had been gripped by the same red-hot tongs with which he himself had formerly tweaked the nose of Nicholas.

Bill then departed but soon found that in consequence of the inflammable materials which strong drink had thrown into his nose, that organ immediately took fire, and, indeed, to tell the truth, kept burning night and day, winter and summer, without ever once going out from that hour to this.

Such was the sad fate of Billy Dawson, who has been walking without stop or stay, from place to place, ever since; and in consequence of the flame on his nose, and his beard being tangled like a wisp of hay, he has been christened by the country folk Will-O'-the-Wisp, while, as it were, to show the mischief of his disposition, the circulating knave, knowing that he must seek the coldest bogs and quagmires in order to cool his nose, seizes upon that opportunity of misleading the unthinking and tipsy night travelers from their way, just that he may have the satisfaction of still taking in as many as possible.